William Kotzwinkle, Glenn Murray, and Elizabeth Gundy

Walter the Farting Dog
Banned from the Beach

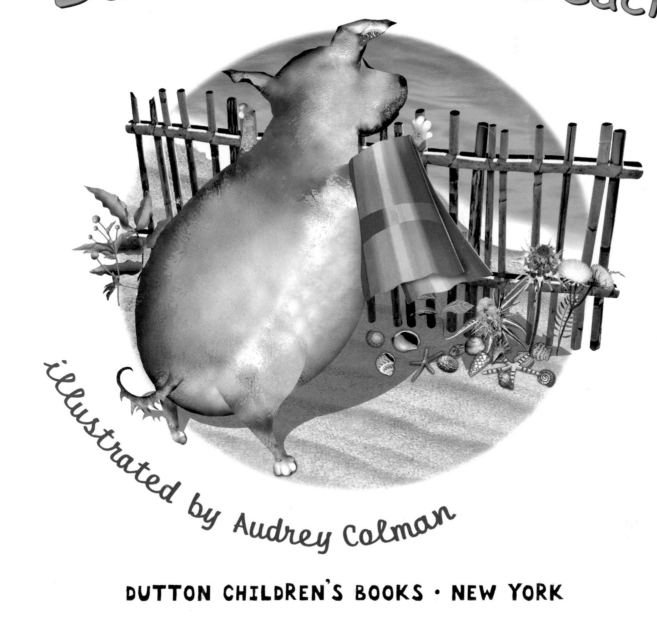

illustrated by Audrey Colman

DUTTON CHILDREN'S BOOKS · NEW YORK

DUTTON CHILDREN'S BOOKS
A division of Penguin Young Readers Group

Published by the Penguin Group
Penguin Group (USA) Inc., 375 Hudson Street, New York, New York 10014, U.S.A. · Penguin Group
(Canada), 90 Eglinton Avenue East, Suite 700, Toronto, Ontario, Canada M4P 2Y3
(a division of Pearson Penguin Canada Inc.) · Penguin Books Ltd, 80 Strand, London WC2R ORL,
England · Penguin Ireland, 25 St Stephen's Green, Dublin 2, Ireland (a division of Penguin Books Ltd)
Penguin Group (Australia), 250 Camberwell Road, Camberwell, Victoria 3124, Australia
(a division of Pearson Australia Group Pty Ltd) · Penguin Books India Pvt Ltd, 11 Community Centre,
Panchsheel Park, New Delhi—110 017, India · Penguin Group (NZ), 67 Apollo Drive, Mairangi Bay,
Auckland 1311, New Zealand (a division of Pearson New Zealand Ltd) · Penguin Books (South Africa)
(Pty) Ltd, 24 Sturdee Avenue, Rosebank, Johannesburg 2196, South Africa · Penguin Books Ltd,
Registered Offices: 80 Strand, London WC2R ORL, England

Published in the United States by Dutton Children's Books,
a division of Penguin Young Readers Group
345 Hudson Street, New York, New York 10014
www.penguin.com/youngreaders

Designed by Jason Henry
Manufactured in China ∗ First Edition
ISBN: 978-0-525-47812-6
1 3 5 7 9 10 8 6 4 2

For everyone who's ever felt
misjudged or misunderstood

Mr. and Mrs. Crabbe were having a ton of fun. There was sand and sea and sunshine every day. There was swimming and snorkeling and parasailing and lots of staff to boss around.

"You there!" called Mrs. Crabbe to the pool attendant. "Get that leaf out of the water."

"And bring us some fresh towels," said Mr. Crabbe. "Make it snappy."

"If only that dog weren't ruining my view," said Mrs. Crabbe.

In the quaint little village, lights twinkled in the trees. Everyone was enjoying the gentle breeze and the sweet smells of the tropical night.

Walter was enjoying himself, too. *Travel broadens a dog's mind,* he thought, farting philosophically.

The Crabbes were sitting nearby at a sidewalk café, complaining about their Key lime pie. Mrs. Crabbe counted the problems on her fingers. "It's not big enough. It's not green enough. It's not sweet enough."

"Or maybe it's *too* sweet," said Mr. Crabbe, smacking his lips.

A pelican flapped its wings at Walter, and Walter farted in alarm. The power of Walter's fart blew the meringue off Mr. Crabbe's pie. It landed in his face and made an awful mess.

The Crabbes glared at Walter. "That dog is ruining our vacation."

Next morning, Father got a phone call from the chief of police.

"I've had serious complaints about your dog," said the chief. "I'm afraid we can't allow him on our streets."

Father hung up. "Sorry, Walter. You're banned from the village."

"But where can Walter go now?" asked Billy.

"He's grounded," said Father. "He stays inside."

"That's not a very nice vacation for Walter," said Betty.

Walter farted.

"Need I say more?" asked Father.

When everyone went out to have fun, Walter stayed inside with his nose pressed against the window.

Well, thought Walter, *I'll just have to make the best of it.*

He sniffed around for something to eat and found a sack of strange-looking tropical fruit. The label said COOK THOROUGHLY. DO NOT EAT RAW! Since Walter couldn't read, he ate it anyway.

Then he went to snooze in the sunshine pouring through the window.

Betty and Billy were building a sandcastle on the beach.

"Look," said Betty, pointing out to sea. "How did that island get there? It wasn't there before."

"It must've been underwater," said Billy. "Now that the tide is out, we can get there. Let's go!"

They waded out through the shallow water to explore the mysterious island.

"This is the sort of place where you find buried treasure," said Billy, beginning to dig.

Suddenly something shiny glittered in the sunlight.

"I knew it!" yelled Billy, holding up a nickel.

"We're rich!" yelled Betty.

Mr. Crabbe sat up under his new beach umbrella. "Those nasty children seem to have found something."

The Crabbes waded out to the little island.

"Let me help you," said Mr. Crabbe, pushing Billy aside.

Mr. Crabbe found a rusty old key and waved it triumphantly. "I have a feeling that this will unlock something very important," he said. Sure enough, ten minutes later, he dug up a door, and the key fit perfectly.

"Maybe we'll find a whole vacation house!" said Betty.

Though they dug for hours, they didn't find anything else, and they didn't notice that their island was shrinking. The tide was rising fast, and the waves began to lap at their feet.

Betty looked up and gasped. "How did the beach get so far away?"

"It's the tide," cried Billy. "We're marooned."

"Out of my way!" shouted Mr. Crabbe and leaped into the water. Mrs. Crabbe dove in after him, followed by Betty and Billy.

They swam as hard as they could, but the undertow was too strong. The current swirled them around and dumped them back on their shrinking little island.

"Our only hope is to build a raft," said Mr. Crabbe.

Walter woke from his nap with a bad feeling. *Betty and Billy must be in trouble!*

Walter's stomach was rumbling like a volcano from the tropical fruit that should have been thoroughly cooked, but he ignored it and raced to the screen door.

Locked!

He stepped back and charged, bursting through the screen and leaving a Walter-shaped hole in the door.

Walter ran to the beach and saw four figures in the distance with the water rising around them. Mr. and Mrs. Crabbe were launching their raft. Billy was trying to help Betty. All Walter could see of Betty was her little head above the surface and her arms waving frantically.

Walter plunged into the surf. Shooting pains twisted him around and flung him back onto the beach.

Was it a cramp from swimming too soon after eating?

No, it was the tropical fruit that should have been thoroughly cooked.

"Walter, save us!" cried Billy.

Walter struggled to rise, but the gases produced by the tropical fruit that should have been thoroughly cooked chose this moment to erupt with terrible force. The tropical-fruit fart produced a boom that was heard along the coast for miles. Coconuts blew off the trees, and the Crabbes, clutching their new umbrella, were blown all the way to the Sandwich Islands.

The waves parted around the little island where Betty and Billy were stranded. Layer upon layer of sand and shells were pushed aside, leaving a pathway across the ocean floor.

Betty and Billy ran toward shore. Halfway there, Billy tripped on something jutting from the ocean floor. Walter raced out to help him.

"It's a treasure chest," cried Billy.

Bones, thought Walter, and grabbed a handle in his teeth. He dragged the chest to the beach. Betty and Billy pried it open.

Walter was disappointed to see that it only contained jewels and gold.